THE CARD

If you want to be successful in life, what do you need? Do you need to be clever, good-looking, kind, hard-working, honest? Or just lucky?

Denry Machin is a cheerful kind of fellow. When he meets a problem, he doesn't lie down and cry about it. He looks for a chance, and when he sees one, he takes it with both hands. He has a lot of luck too, of course. It's lucky that the Countess decides to give a ball, but how does Denry manage to get an invitation? It's lucky that Mrs Codleyn has an argument with Denry's employer, but how does Denry become Mrs Codleyn's rent-collector? And it's very lucky indeed for Denry when the *Hjalmar* goes down in the sea off Llandudno – but how does Denry make a thousand pounds out of it?

The people of Bursley, the town where Denry lives, love a young man who makes them laugh. 'He's a real card,' they say. They can't wait to hear about his next adventure . . .

OXFORD BOOKWORMS LIBRARY

Human Interest

The Card

Stage 3 (1000 headwords)

Series Editor: Jennifer Bassett
Founder Editor: Tricia Hedge
Activities Editors: Jennifer Bassett and Christine Lindop

ARNOLD BENNETT

The Card

Retold by
Nick Bullard

Illustrated by
Simon Gurr

OXFORD UNIVERSITY PRESS

OXFORD

UNIVERSITY PRESS

Great Clarendon Street, Oxford OX2 6DP

Oxford University Press is a department of the University of Oxford.
It furthers the University's objective of excellence in research, scholarship,
and education by publishing worldwide in

Oxford New York

Auckland Cape Town Dar es Salaam Hong Kong Karachi
Kuala Lumpur Madrid Melbourne Mexico City Nairobi
New Delhi Shanghai Taipei Toronto

With offices in

Argentina Austria Brazil Chile Czech Republic France Greece
Guatemala Hungary Italy Japan Poland Portugal Singapore
South Korea Switzerland Thailand Turkey Ukraine Vietnam

OXFORD and OXFORD ENGLISH are registered trade marks of
Oxford University Press in the UK and in certain other countries

ISBN 978 0 19 479111 3

Printed in Hong Kong

Word count (main text): 11,100 words

For more information on the Oxford Bookworms Library,
visit www.oup.com/elt/bookworms

CONTENTS

STORY INTRODUCTION   i

1 The dance   1

2 The rent collector and the Widow Hullins   10

3 The dancing teacher and the furniture van   18

4 Saved by a storm   25

5 The rescue of the Countess   35

6 The battle with Denry's mother   44

7 The mayor, the wife, and the football club   49

GLOSSARY   57

ACTIVITIES: Before Reading   60

ACTIVITIES: While Reading   61

ACTIVITIES: After Reading   64

ABOUT THE AUTHOR   68

ABOUT THE BOOKWORMS LIBRARY   69

THE DANCE

Edward Henry Machin first saw daylight on the 27th of May, 1867, in Brougham Street in Bursley, the oldest of the Five Towns. Brougham Street goes down a hill to the canal, and contains a number of potbanks or pottery factories as well as some small houses. The rent for one of these houses was not high – only about twenty-three pence a week.

Edward Henry's mother (his father was dead) lived by making and washing clothes for fine ladies. She did not often laugh, and if you tried to argue with her, you never got very far. She was a woman of few words, and saved time every day by calling her son Denry, instead of Edward Henry.

Denry did not work hard at school, and boys who were lazy and not very clever usually just found jobs in the potbanks. Luckily, at the age of twelve, he won a place at the best school in Bursley. It happened like this. On the second day of the examination, Denry arrived a little early. As he walked around the examination room, he came to the teacher's desk, where he saw a list of names with the marks for the first day of the examination. The highest possible mark was thirty, but next to his name he saw the number 7. The numbers were written in pencil, and the pencil was on the desk. He picked it up, looked around the empty room, and at the door, and then

1

wrote a 2 in front of the 7. Of course, this was not honest, but how many truly honest schoolboys are there? Denry was no worse than most of them.

Denry did not do well at his new school, but he did not do badly either – and he was usually very pleased with himself. As he grew older, he continued to think well of himself. He knew that he was made for better things than a job in the potbanks, working with his hands.

*   *   *

When Denry was sixteen, his mother made a very fine dress for Mr Duncalf's sister. Mr Duncalf was the most important lawyer in Bursley. His sister was grateful to Mrs Machin, and so Denry got a job in Mr Duncalf's office. For several years Denry was happy. Then he met the Countess.

The Countess of Chell was a very grand lady. Her husband was one of the richest men in the Five Towns and was the new Mayor of Bursley. The mayor and his wife had decided to have a ball and to invite all the most important people in the town. There were thirty-five thousand people in Bursley, and at least two thousand of these thought that they were important. But only two hundred could dance in the Town Hall.

Three weeks and three days before the ball, Denry was sitting, alone, in Mr Duncalf's office when a tall and pretty young woman walked in. Before Denry could hide the newspaper he was reading, she said 'Good morning' in a very friendly way.

'Good morning, madam,' answered Denry.

*Denry looked around the empty room, and then
wrote a 2 in front of the 7.*

'Is Mr Duncalf in?'

'No, madam. He's at the Town Hall.'

'Well, just tell him I called.'

'Of course, madam. Nothing I can do?'

She was already turning away, but she turned back and
gave him a smile. 'Could you give him this list? The other lists
are coming to him as well. The invitations must go out by
Wednesday.'

She was gone. It was the first time Denry had seen the Countess, and she was even more beautiful than her photographs. And so easy to talk to! He started looking at her list of names, and he had a fantastic idea. He could go to the ball himself. The Countess had made a list of people to invite, but she had asked four or five other people for lists as well. She wanted Mr Duncalf to put the lists together and send the invitations. Of course the work was given to Denry, so it was easy to add E. H. Machin to the list. On Wednesday Denry received his invitation, and on Thursday he accepted it.

*   *   *

Denry had never been to a ball. He couldn't dance and he didn't have an evening suit. All the rich young men of Bursley bought their suits at Shillitoe's, so two days later Denry stepped into Shillitoe's shop. 'I want you to make me an evening suit,' he said to young Shillitoe.

Shillitoe knew Denry and he also knew that Denry did not have enough money to pay for a suit. He replied that he was too busy. 'So you're going to the ball, are you?' he asked, surprised.

'Yes,' said Denry; 'are you?'

Shillitoe shook his head. 'I've no time for balls.'

Denry looked around the shop, and at the door, and then said, 'I can get you an invitation if you like.'

Denry got his suit, and two years to pay for it.

One of the best dancing teachers in Bursley was Miss Ruth Earp. Denry learned to dance quickly, but he paid nothing for his lessons. Miss Earp also got an invitation to the ball.

4

Miss Earp was not beautiful, but she was young and a very good dancer, and at his last lesson Denry asked, 'Will you give me the first dance at the ball?'

Ruth Earp thought for a minute, and then said yes.

* * *

It took Denry two hours to get ready for the ball, and he arrived a little late. He walked up the beautiful double staircase into the ballroom and looked for Ruth. When he found her, he asked, 'What about that first dance?'

'It's nearly finished,' she answered, coldly.

'I'm awfully sorry. Can we finish it?'

'No!' she said, and walked away.

She was angry with him, and Denry did not know what to say. But she was only at the ball, he thought, because he had got her invitation for her!

He joined a group of young men who were watching the dancing. Harold Etches, who was one of the richest young men in the Five Towns, was there, with two or three of the Swetnam boys, and Shillitoe. At first Denry did not say anything. They all knew, of course, that he was Mr Duncalf's office worker and the son of a washer-woman, but all young men – rich or poor – look the same in evening suits.

The conversation in the group was about the Countess. All the important older men in the town were standing around her, but she was not dancing. Perhaps she didn't want to, but perhaps they were all afraid to ask.

'Why doesn't someone ask her to dance?' asked Denry suddenly.

'Why doesn't somebody ask her to dance?' asked Denry.

'Why don't you?' said Shillitoe. 'It's a free country.'

'Perhaps I will,' Denry said.

Harold Etches looked at Denry for a moment. '*You* won't ask her,' he said. Then he smiled, not very pleasantly. 'I'll give you five pounds if you do.'

'All right,' said Denry, and quickly walked away.

6

'She can't eat me! She can't eat me!' he said to himself as he walked towards the Countess. The men were still around her and one of them, Denry saw, was Mr Duncalf. Denry was sorry about this because Mr Duncalf didn't know, of course, that Denry was coming to the ball.

Suddenly he found himself standing in front of the Countess, and immediately he forgot all the fine, polite words that Ruth Earp had taught him.

'Could I have this dance with you?' he said quickly, but smiling and showing his teeth. ('I've won that fiver, Mr Etches!' he said to himself.)

The Countess had to accept. She could see that everyone else was afraid to ask – and she did want to dance! So they danced together, and all the men of Bursley watched with open mouths. Denry managed to dance well most of the time, although once they nearly hit two other dancers. When the music stopped, the Countess looked at Denry and saw that he was really just a boy.

'You dance well!' she said, smiling almost like an aunt.

'Do I?' he smiled back. 'It's the first time I've ever danced, except in a lesson.'

'Really? You pick things up easily, I suppose.'

'Yes,' he said. 'Do you?'

Something in Denry's question amused the Countess very much. She put her head back and laughed, and everybody in the room could see that Denry had made the Countess laugh. She was still laughing, and so was he, when he thanked her for the dance.

As she turned away, Denry saw that she had dropped her fan. Quickly, he picked it up and put it in his pocket. Then he walked back to the group of young men.

'Here you are!' said Harold Etches, giving Denry a five-pound note.

'You do pick things up easily, don't you?' said the Countess.

Denry just smiled, and put the note in his pocket. He could see in the faces of the young men around him that he was suddenly famous. He was no longer just the son of a washer-woman; he was the man who had first danced with the Countess.

'Just the same as dancing with any other woman,' he said, when Shillitoe asked him what it was like.

'What was she laughing at?' someone asked.

'Ah!' said Denry. 'I can't tell you that.'

This was not the last time he was asked that question, but he always refused to answer. Many young ladies wanted to dance with him now, after his success with the Countess. Later, he saw Ruth Earp again and danced with her, and with her young friend, Nellie. But he said nothing at all about the Countess's fan in his pocket.

At the end of the ball, just as the Countess was leaving, Denry pushed through the crowd and held out her fan.

'I've just picked it up,' he said to the Countess.

'Oh! Thank you so much!' she said. Then she smiled. 'You do pick things up easily, don't you?'

And both Denry and the Countess laughed and laughed, but nobody in Bursley knew why.

Denry walked home that night in a dream, thinking about the Countess, Ruth Earp and Nellie, and about the five-pound note in his pocket – more than he got for a month's work in Mr Duncalf's office.

He was a happy man. But trouble was waiting for him.

THE RENT COLLECTOR
AND THE WIDOW HULLINS

The ball made a new man of Denry. He had danced with the
Countess – the first man to dance with her. Bursley thought
he was a wonderful fellow, and so did Denry himself. He had
always been a hopeful, cheerful kind of person. Now he was
filled with happiness all the time, and when he got out of bed
in the morning, he felt like singing and dancing. Something
good was going to happen, he knew; he just had to wait. He
didn't have to wait very long.

A few days after the ball, Mrs Codleyn came to see Mr
Duncalf. Mrs Codleyn was a widow, a woman of nearly sixty.
She owned about seventy small houses in Bursley, and Mr
Duncalf collected the rents for her. (Denry, of course, actually
went to the houses to get the money.) Although the rent from
all these houses was about twelve pounds a week, Mrs
Codleyn always said that it was not enough. And the taxes!
Every year the taxes on those houses got higher and higher,
and Mrs Codleyn hated paying her taxes.

Mr Duncalf was an important man at the Town Hall.
Because of this, Mrs Codleyn thought that he should make the
taxes lower on her houses. Mrs Codleyn had chosen Mr

Duncalf to collect her rents because she thought he was an honest man – but an honest man would never try to change the taxes specially for one person. What strange ideas people have sometimes!

Mrs Codleyn had just heard that her taxes were going up again, but she did not stay long in Mr Duncalf's office. The conversation (which Denry listened to through the wall) was short, loud, and not very polite. When Mrs Codleyn left, Mr Duncalf called Denry into his office.

The conversation was short, loud, and not very polite.

'Write this letter to Mrs Codleyn,' he said angrily. '*Madam, I understand from our conversation this morning that you prefer to find another lawyer . . .*'

Denry wrote down the letter. As he was leaving the room, Mr Duncalf spoke again.

'Machin!'

Denry knew what was coming. He had known it was coming ever since the ball.

'Who invited you to the ball?'

There it was. A very difficult question.

'I did, sir.' Denry just could not think of a lie.

'Why?'

'I thought perhaps you'd forgotten to, sir.'

'I suppose you think you're a really fine fellow after your dance with the Countess?' Mr Duncalf said unpleasantly.

'Yes,' said Denry. 'Do *you*?'

He had not meant to say it. The same little question had amused the Countess greatly, but it was true to say that it was not amusing his employer now. Mr Duncalf's own dance with the Countess had come to a very quick ending, because he had stepped heavily on her skirt.

'You will leave my office at the end of the week,' said Mr Duncalf, coldly.

'Oh, very well,' said Denry. And he said to himself: 'Something good *must* happen now.' He had no idea what he would do next, but he was still cheerful. And he still had Harold Etches' five pounds.

The next morning both Mrs Codleyn and Denry were late

for church. Mrs Codleyn was late by accident and also because she was fat. Denry was late because he had planned it that way. The two met at the church door.

'Well, you're nice people, I must say!' Mrs Codleyn said to Denry. She meant Duncalf and all his office workers.

'Nothing to do with me, you know!' said Denry.

'I wish I could find someone else to collect my rents.'

'I can still collect them for you, if you like,' said Denry.

'You?'

'I've told Duncalf I'm leaving him,' Denry said. 'The fact is, he and I don't agree on a lot of things.'

Mrs Codleyn looked at him and thought about it. He was just a young office worker, and his mother was a washerwoman. His suit was clean, but old and unfashionable.

'And what's more,' Denry went on, 'I'll do the work for less money. You pay Duncalf ninety pence a week – well, I'll do it for sixty pence a week. And I'll collect them better than him. Give me a month and you'll see the difference!'

At the end of the week a notice appeared on the front door of Denry's mother's house, which said:

E. H. MACHIN

Rent Collector

In a few weeks, Denry was doing very well. He was working for himself, and in two days he earned more money than in a week with Mr Duncalf. He walked around the town, smiling, looking important, talking to other young men, and thinking of new ways of making money.

*　*　*

One Monday morning he went to Mrs Hullins' house to collect the rent. It was a very small house, not much more than one room downstairs and one room upstairs. The rent was fifteen pence a week, and the Widow Hullins had not paid any rent at all for some weeks. She had lived there all her life, and after two husbands and eleven children, she now lived alone. She had seen a lot of life, and was old and tired.

'I've nothing for you,' she said when Denry came in.

'That's not good enough, I'm afraid,' said Denry cheerfully. 'I'm not leaving until I get ten pence.'

'It'll be a long wait. I'll have nothing until Saturday, when my son Jack starts a new job.'

'I'm sorry,' said Denry kindly, 'but if you don't pay, you'll have to go. Mrs Codleyn will put you out in the street, you know. Why don't you go and live with one of your children?'

After some more conversation, Denry left the house, still smiling cheerfully. And then, two minutes later, he put his head round the door again.

'Look here, mother,' he said, 'I'll lend you ten pence if you like. But you must pay me a penny a week for it. You must pay me back next week and give me eleven pence.'

And he wrote down *'Ten pence, paid'* in her rent book.

'Eh, you're a funny fellow, Mr Machin,' said Mrs Hullins.

The next Monday, all the neighbours knew that Denry could be very helpful about problems with the rent. And Denry, with his cheerful, smiling face, saved many families from a life in the street. Of course, it was good business for

'I'll lend you ten pence if you like,' said Denry.

him, too. If someone borrowed ten pence for four weeks, when they paid Denry back, they had to give him fourteen pence. If it was for six months, they had to pay him back thirty-six pence. Money made like this just grows and grows.

Denry began to think that he was different from other men. He had invited himself to the ball, danced with the Countess, left his job with Duncalf, taken Duncalf's rent-collecting, and then introduced the idea of collecting rents and lending money at the same time. He was becoming well-known in Bursley as an unusual and amusing fellow – in other words, a card.

But then the day came when Mrs Codleyn decided to sell some of her smaller houses. This was very bad news for Denry because these houses were the most important part of his business. Denry talked to her, and tried to show her that it was not a sensible idea, but it was no good. Finally, Denry said wildly that he would buy some of the houses himself.

'I'll buy the Widow Hullins' house,' he said. 'I'll give you forty-five pounds for it.' It was all the money he had.

Mrs Codleyn agreed. And selling this one house, for the moment, seemed to be enough for her.

* * *

Denry was now a property owner. And he had also joined the Sports Club – the club for the rich, the fashionable, and the successful men of Bursley. It was a great thing for the son of a washer-woman to join a club like this.

On Denry's second visit to the club, he saw that some of the most important men in Bursley were there. A group of them were arguing in a corner of the comfortable bar.

'Some of the poor people in this town live in the most terrible old houses,' said Charles Fearns, a lawyer. 'And the town just doesn't care about them. There's an old woman – Hullins is her name – who's lived in the same awful old house for fifty years. She pays fifteen pence a week rent for this place, and now she's going to be put out into the street because she can't pay.'

'Who's the hard-hearted owner?' someone asked.

'Mrs Codleyn,' said Fearns.

'Mrs Codleyn isn't the owner,' called Denry, who was sitting at the next table, smiling. 'I am.'

'Oh, I'm sorry,' said Fearns, 'I had no idea—'

'Not at all!' said Denry. 'But what can I do? She can't pay, or doesn't want to pay. Do I let her live in the house for no rent because she's seventy? Come on, tell me. What do I do?'

'Fearns would make her a present of the house!' a voice said laughing, and everybody else laughed too.

'Well, that's what I'll do,' said Denry. 'I'll give her the house. That's the kind of hard-hearted owner I am.'

The room was silent for a moment.

'I mean it!' said Denry, and picked up his glass. 'She can have the house! Good health to the Widow Hullins.'

And the next morning, everybody in Bursley was talking about it. 'I say, have you heard Machin's latest?'

He was now not just a card; he was *the* card.

THE DANCING TEACHER
AND THE FURNITURE VAN

One day in July Denry knocked at the door of a house at the top of Brougham Street. The dancing teacher, Miss Ruth Earp, lived there, in a house owned by Mr Calvert, and Denry now collected Mr Calvert's rents for him.

'Good morning, Miss Earp,' said Denry, when she opened the door. 'I've come about the rent.'

'The rent?' said Ruth, surprised. She gave him a look which seemed to say, 'Why does a little boy like you ask about my rent?'

'Yes. I collect rents for Mr Calvert now,' Denry said. He did not like the 'little boy' look on her face, and added, 'You haven't paid any rent for more than a year.'

Ruth Earp gave a hard little laugh. 'I see,' she said. 'So Mr Herbert Calvert is paying you to do his dirty work now. I must tell you, Mr Machin, that not long ago Mr Calvert was more interested in me than in my rent. But when I decided that I could not return his interest, he said things which hurt me very much – very much indeed.'

'Oh,' said Denry. He told himself that he was here on business.

'But if you can't pay your rent, Miss Earp, I'm afraid you'll have to leave.'

Ruth looked at him, and then gave a slow, sad smile. 'Of course I can pay it,' she said gently. 'I just wanted to punish Mr Calvert a little. I can't pay you just at this moment, I'm afraid. The bank is closed. Can you come back tomorrow? Come at four o'clock, and I'll give you a cup of tea.'

The next day Denry returned. It was the first time he had taken tea with a young lady, and so he had put on his best summer suit. He noticed that Ruth was wearing a very pretty dress – something white with bits of pink in it.

Ruth had introduced Denry to dancing, and now she introduced him to taking tea. It was all very beautifully done – tea in very small cups, little squares of bread-and-butter, and interesting conversation. Ruth seemed much more friendly today, and Denry found it all very pleasant.

Then suddenly Ruth stopped speaking, and lay back in her chair with her eyes closed.

'Is something the matter?' asked Denry.

'I'm afraid I've got an awful headache,' she answered.

'I'm sorry,' said Denry. 'Is there anything I can do? Perhaps you should lie down. Would you like me to go?'

'But I must pay you the rent first.' She put her hand to her head. 'The money's in that desk. Could you get it for me?'

She gave Denry a key. He went over to the desk, put the key in the lock, and tried to turn it. Nothing happened, and then the key turned and turned. 'I can't open it,' he said.

Ruth stood up, holding her head. She came over to the desk,

and tried the key. 'Oh dear. I'm afraid you've broken the lock. I'll have to get someone to mend it tomorrow morning, and then I'll bring the money round to you.'

'Don't worry,' said Denry. 'I can easily call back for it tomorrow. And I'm very sorry about the lock.'

*   *   *

Late that night Denry came home from an evening at the Sports Club and just as he reached his mother's house, he saw something strange at the top end of Brougham Street. A large furniture van was moving down the street all on its own; there

Suddenly Ruth lay back in her chair with her eyes closed.

were no horses. Clearly, the owner had left it there and forgotten to put on the brakes. It was moving slowly now, but Denry could see that when it reached the bottom of Brougham Street, it could be very dangerous.

Denry was always at his finest at difficult or dangerous moments. As the van passed him, moving at about five or six kilometres an hour, he jumped on, losing his hat, and tried to put the brakes on. For a second or two the van seemed to slow down, but then Denry realized that the brakes were not working and the van was moving faster and faster down the hill. At the bottom of the street was the canal, and clearly nothing was going to stop the van now. It was too late to jump off, so Denry closed his eyes and held on hard.

When the van went in, Denry was under water for a moment, but then he managed to climb further up on the front of the van. Everything was still and dark, except for a little starlight on the water. Only Denry had seen the van's strange journey down the hill.

'Well, well!' he said aloud to himself.

And a voice answered from inside the van: 'Who's there?'

Denry's heart seemed to stop beating. 'It's me!' he said.

'Not Mr Machin?' said the voice.

'Yes,' said he. 'I jumped on as it came down the street – and here we are!'

'Oh!' cried the voice. 'I wish you could get round to me.'

It was Ruth Earp's voice. Denry understood immediately. Ruth had played with him! She had planned to take her furniture and run away in the night. She had no rent money

21

locked in her desk at all. But he was not angry with her, just amused. Ruth was really very clever – in fact, very like Denry himself.

He had to climb over the roof of the van to get to the back. The van was black inside, and the floor was under fifty centimetres of water.

'Where are you?'

'I'm here. I'm on a table. It's the only thing the men put in the van before they went to have their supper.'

Denry felt around until he touched her wet dress.

'You're a bad girl, you know,' he said.

Ruth started to cry. 'I know,' she said miserably. 'But I had no money. What could I do?'

Denry climbed on to the table next to her.

'What can we do now?' she whispered.

'Wait until it gets light,' said he.

So they waited. On a hot July night it is not unpleasant to sit in the dark with your feet in water. Ruth told Denry all about her life and her money problems.

When it started to get light, Denry saw that the back of the van was only a metre from the edge of the canal, so they jumped. In the grey early light they looked at one another. Ruth had a black eye, and Denry had lost his hat.

'Go home by the back streets, not up Brougham Street,' said Denry. 'I'll come and see you in the morning.'

It was four o'clock in the morning when Denry went quietly up his mother's stairs. He had seen nobody.

*　*　*

Ruth had a black eye, and Denry had lost his hat.

Only two people in Bursley ever knew exactly what had happened that night. Everybody knew that Denry had tried to save the town from a dangerous runaway van and had ended in the canal. But as well as this one fact, there were a great many stories about the accident, and in these stories the names of Denry and Ruth were always appearing.

One morning Denry went to see Mr Herbert Calvert and gave him ten pounds which he said came from Ruth Earp.

Calvert gave Denry a strange look. 'What's going on?' he asked. 'Is it true that she was trying to leave without paying?'

'I don't think so. It's all very extraordinary. I think the van was at the wrong house.'

'Are you engaged to her?' asked Calvert.

Denry waited for a moment. 'Yes,' he said. 'Are you?'

And Denry thought to himself that few engagements had begun as strangely as theirs.

4

SAVED BY A STORM

When newly engaged people like Denry and Ruth want to go away on a summer holiday, there are many things to think about. A businessman, for example, who lives by collecting rents every week cannot go away easily for two. And a young woman who lives alone must always be careful about what other people think, so Ruth asked her friend Nellie Cotterill to go with her.

Ruth and Nellie took a room together at 26 St Asaph's Road, Llandudno. Denry took a room at number 28 St Asaph's Road. Who could want more?

Denry had never seen the sea before. As he walked along the beach in his best clothes, with the girls on either side of him, he thought it was all wonderful. He also saw fantastic possibilities for making money, because here were fifty thousand people, all on holiday, all wanting to do interesting things, and all with money to spend.

Denry thought about this a lot because he felt he was now a serious person. He had something to live for. He was very pleased and happy to be engaged to Ruth, although still a little surprised. What could this fine young lady see in *him*?

They had not discussed money at all, although Denry wanted to. It was clear that Ruth thought he was a rich man, and Denry was spending a lot of money. In fact, he could not move without paying for something. The pier, swimming, ice cream, chairs, fruit, boat trips, photographs, teas, coffees – even a short walk with Ruth was expensive.

Ruth had very little money, but it didn't worry her. She didn't know what money was, and she spent Denry's like water. The gentle, silent Nellie often asked to pay for something herself, but of course Denry couldn't let her. He liked Nellie Cotterill. She thought that he and Ruth were wonderful, and although she was a very quiet person, she was also very sensible.

At the end of the first week Denry was getting more and more worried about money. On the Monday morning he went back to Bursley to collect rents, and returned to Llandudno on Tuesday evening with his pockets full of rent money. Something had to happen, he thought. He didn't know what it was, but three months of engagement with Ruth Earp was going to leave him penniless.

* * *

He was saved by a storm at sea. They woke up on Wednesday morning to find the rain and wind crashing against the windows. The three walked down into the town, where they learnt that the town's lifeboat had gone out to a ship further along the coast. A second lifeboat (an old one, now owned by a fisherman) had gone out to a Norwegian ship, the *Hjalmar*, which was in difficulties just off Llandudno itself. Everyone in the town was watching the lifeboat save the sailors while the ship went down. Denry and the girls went onto the pier, and Denry even got his feet wet helping one or two of the Norwegian sailors from the lifeboat onto the pier. After that, he talked for a time to Cregeen, the owner of the lifeboat.

It was a very exciting day, and it gave Denry an idea.

'I'll write a report about all this for the *Signal*,' he said. This was the Five Towns daily newspaper.

'Oh yes!' said Nellie. 'What a good idea!'

The next morning Denry was up early to send the report off by train. Then he and the girls walked into town – and spent more money. Everybody in the town was talking about

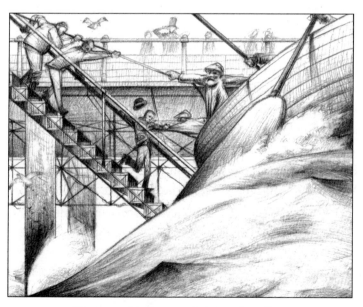

Denry got his feet wet helping the sailors
from the lifeboat onto the pier.

27

the storm, the wreck of the *Hjalmar* and the wonderful rescue of all the Norwegian sailors by the lifeboat.

After a few minutes, Ruth turned to Denry.

'I had the bill for our room this morning,' she said.

'Oh!' he said. 'Did you pay it?'

'Yes. But now I've almost no money left. We spent so much money while you were away in Bursley. You don't know how quickly money goes!' She waited a moment, then said, 'I suppose we'll have to go home.'

'What a pity!' said Denry, sadly.

Of course, Ruth wanted Denry to say that he could pay for her to stay. But all he said was, 'What a pity!'

'I think I'll go home this afternoon.'

'I'm sorry,' said Denry.

At that moment a hand touched his arm. It was Cregeen.

'Mr Machin. It's now or never. It's twenty-five pounds if you can pay today.'

'Right!' said Denry. 'I'll see you this evening.'

Ruth pretended not to be interested in any of this.

* * *

Poor Nellie. She knew something was wrong, but she didn't know what it was. All she knew was that her holiday was coming to a sudden end. In the evening, the three of them walked to the station.

'Where's your luggage?' Ruth asked Denry.

'I'm not going. I've got business here.'

There was a bookshop in the station. Denry bought the *Signal*, which had just come in, and there was his report:

'Terrible Storm in North Wales – a report by Mr E. H. Machin of Bursley'. Denry was ready to explode with happiness, but he gave the newspaper calmly to Ruth.

She did not look at it. 'We'll read it on the train,' she said.

The bookshop also had a lot of souvenirs of Llandudno. Ruth wanted a glass plate with a picture of Great Orme Head on it, but the man in the shop said that they had sold out.

'Couldn't you get one and send it to me?' said Ruth.

'Oh yes,' said the man, taking out a book. 'What name?'

Ruth looked at Denry, in the way that a woman always looks at a man when she wants him to pay.

'Rothschild,' said Denry. 'The millionaire.'

These words ended their engagement. The next day Denry received by post a ring in a box, with a short letter.

'I only said "Rothschild"!' said Denry to himself. But secretly, he was pleased.

* * *

An hour later Denry met Cregeen, and was soon the owner of the old Llandudno lifeboat. He then went to find Simeon, an old sailor with a white beard. He had been in the lifeboat when they rescued the men on the *Hjalmar*.

'I've got the boat,' said Denry. 'I'll give you two pounds for the week.'

'All right,' said the old man. 'And I've seen three of those Norwegians. They don't speak English, but they understand about the money.'

'Good,' said Denry. 'I'll see you tomorrow morning.'

At five o'clock the next morning a boat left Llandudno.

29

There were six men rowing, three of them Norwegians. There was also a man with a white beard, and Denry. In twenty minutes they were at the wreck of the *Hjalmar* and Denry was feeling very ill. Twenty minutes more and he was happy to be back on land.

At ten o'clock that morning two Norwegian sailors were walking around the town giving little notices to everyone they met.

THE WRECK OF THE HJALMAR
FAMOUS RESCUE AT LLANDUDNO
Every day at 11, 12, 2, 3, 4, 5 and 6 o'clock the famous lifeboat which rescued the Norwegian sailors will visit the wreck of the *Hjalmar.* The lifeboat's captain is Simeon Edwards, one of the rescuers, and the lifeboat is rowed by three of the rescued Norwegians.

Return trip, 12 pence

On the first day, Denry made twelve pounds. That evening he received a packet in the post. It was from Nellie. There was a box of chocolates and a note which said: *Thank you very much for the holiday. I hope you will like these. Nellie.* Denry was very pleased by this. Ruth's young friend, he thought, was much more grateful than Ruth herself.

The boat trips out to the wreck became more and more popular. In the afternoons, Denry had to ask 25 pence – it was the only way to stop the big crowds that were waiting on the

30

The boat trips out to the wreck became more and more popular.

beach. Soon, he was making a hundred pounds a week. He was sorry the wreck had happened in August and not July. He was sorry there were not two or even forty *Hjalmars*.

One day in September when business was beginning to slow down (he was down to fifty pounds a week), Denry had a very pleasant surprise. He met Nellie on the beach, and it was a fact that seeing her gave him a great feeling of happiness. She was with her father, Councillor Cotterill, and her mother. The Councillor was a builder who had become rich building cheap houses for the people of the Five Towns.

'Well, young man!' said Councillor Cotterill.

He continued to call Denry 'young man' in a way that made Denry cross. 'I've made more money this summer than you have in a year,' he said silently to the Councillor's back.

'You must have dinner with me one evening,' Denry said finally. 'At the Majestic.' The Majestic was the finest, and most expensive, hotel in Llandudno. Some of the waiters were French!

They agreed to go the next day. Then Mrs Cotterill remembered that Ruth was coming to stay with them for a few days.

'Bring her along too!' said Denry.

The dinner was a great success. Denry had never arranged a dinner before, but it was easy. You just walked into the hotel in the morning and said what you wanted. The hotel arranged everything! And it was easy to meet a woman who had just broken off her engagement to you. You just said, 'Good afternoon, how are you?' and she said the same. Then you shook hands. And there you were, still alive.

After the meal, Denry walked back with the others to their hotel. Councillor Cotterill had stopped calling Denry 'young man'; he now called him 'my boy'.

'That lifeboat. It was just an idea, my boy, just an idea.'

'Yes,' said Denry, 'but I thought of it.'

'The question is,' said the Councillor, 'can you think of any more ideas as good?'

'Well,' said Denry, 'can *you*?'

When they reached the Cotterills' hotel, Ruth waited a moment while the others went in, and then turned to Denry:

'I don't feel like sleeping at all. I suppose you wouldn't like to go for a walk?'

'Well . . .'

'I suppose you're very tired.'

'No,' he replied. 'It's this moonlight I'm afraid of.'

A few days later the Cotterills and Ruth Earp went home, and Denry went with them. He had now sold the lifeboat and brought all his business in Llandudno to an end. He had very little luggage, but he did have a new hat-box. It was very heavy.

When Denry got home, he was pleased to see his mother again. She had often collected his rents for him during the summer, and had done it very well. He gave the hat-box to her, and she immediately dropped it.

'I don't want any of your games, young man,' she said crossly. 'What's in it?'

'Some pretty stones from the beach.'

She picked up the hat-box, opened it, and screamed. It fell to the floor with a crash and Mrs Machin was standing up to her

33

The hat-box fell to the floor with a crash.

ankles in money. She could see coins running all over the floor. At last they stopped moving, and then it was silent. Denry could hear his heart beating. For once in her life his mother could not find a word to say.

For several days afterwards Mrs Machin was still picking up coins. The story of the money in the hat-box quickly went round the town. It was Denry's 'latest' and people talked about it for weeks afterwards.

5

THE RESCUE OF THE COUNTESS

Denry's rent-collecting business grew and grew. He had come back from the Llandudno adventure with a thousand pounds. Two years later he had two thousand pounds, and his bank manager spoke to him with great politeness. Denry now rented a small office, and employed an office-boy.

He also bought a mule and cart. He said he needed them for his work. He could, of course, collect rents on a bicycle, and a bicycle doesn't eat much, or run away. But Denry wanted a mule. It was a good advertisement for his business.

Denry was happy that people talked about the mule as his 'latest', and he was happy to be making money. But he wanted more than money. He always looking for new ideas, exciting things to do – things which would make sure that he was always the greatest 'card' in the Five Towns.

One day, a new notice appeared on Denry's door:

FIVE TOWNS SAVINGS CLUB

Secretary and Manager – E. H. Machin

Many shops in the Five Towns had savings clubs. Every week customers paid a few pence into the club. At Christmas the customers could spend all the money they had paid in. Denry's idea was for a savings club for every shop in the Five Towns. It was a fantastic idea. A poor person could pay just a little money every week, and to make it easier, Denry could come to the house and collect the money. Denry's savings club was special in one very important way. After paying a pound to Denry, someone could spend *two* pounds in the shops immediately – although they must then, of course, continue to pay into the club every week.

Denry needed to make a profit, of course, and his profit would come from the shops. For every six pence spent in a shop, the shop had to pay him one penny. He started by going to Bostocks, the biggest clothes shop in the Five Towns. With Bostocks' name on the list it was easier to find other shops. In two weeks he had nearly a hundred.

Now he needed something to give the club a good start. For twenty-five pounds Denry could put an advertisement on the front page of the *Signal*, but he preferred free advertisements. Then he had an idea. He could ask the Countess of Chell to be the patron of his club. Hers was the best possible name to have at the top of his letter paper. She was the richest woman in the Five Towns. Some people loved her and some people hated her, but everybody knew her.

'I'll ask her. I'll have her as a patron,' he said to himself. 'I'll go to Sneyd Hall. She can't eat me.'

So one morning he arrived, without his mule, at the home of the Countess of Chell. He had been to Sneyd Hall before; the gardens were open to the people of the Five Towns, and there were often hundreds of people there on Sunday afternoons in summer. But today the gardens were empty.

It was a long walk between the trees up to the house, and a

long walk up the steps. Denry rang, and the door opened.

'Well?' said a lady. She was dressed in black.

'Can I see the Countess?' he asked, giving her his card.

'I will ask,' she answered. She disappeared into the house, leaving Denry in the hall.

A few moments later he heard the Countess's voice:

'Oh, no! I'm terribly busy. I'm leaving in a few minutes.'

Still Denry waited. Nobody came to see him. Minutes passed and still nothing. Had they forgotten him? Then, through an open door in the back of the house he saw a man. It was Jock, the son of a friend of his mother. Jock worked at Sneyd Hall, where he drove the Countess's carriage.

Denry did not want to shout through the house, so he walked towards him. 'Jock!' he called, softly.

Jock didn't hear, and disappeared through another door. Denry followed, through door after door, until suddenly he found himself in a long ballroom, full of mirrors, paintings and rich furniture, with high windows to one side and big doors on the other. Jock had disappeared. Denry tried the big doors, but they were all locked. He went back to the door he had used to come into the room. But strangely, that was now locked as well. Then he heard horses outside, and running to a window, he saw the Countess's carriage driving away.

Denry tried knocking on all the doors, first politely, then noisily. He tried calling out, then shouting as loudly as he could. Nothing. At last he realized that there was nobody to hear him. He was a prisoner in an empty house.

He looked around the room. The only possible escape was to

break a window, so Denry preferred to wait until night. He spent a long afternoon in the great ballroom of Sneyd Hall, looking at pictures and furniture. When night fell, he broke one of the big windows and went home. The Five Towns Savings Club began life without the Countess.

The next morning, Denry opened the *Signal* and suddenly felt very ill.

ROBBERY AT SNEYD HALL

Yesterday, thieves broke into the great ballroom at Sneyd, home of the Countess of Chell. The police say that nothing seems to be missing. The Countess (who is away in Italy) will pay twenty pounds for any information about the thieves.

Denry was lucky. The robbery was the talk of the town for a few days, but nobody, it seemed, had remembered his visit to Sneyd Hall, or found his visiting card. And because nothing was stolen, the police were not very interested. Indeed, a week or two later, Denry saw a chance to make something out of his adventure. All that long afternoon he had been in the great ballroom, and he had used his eyes well. He remembered everything. Soon, a report appeared in the *Signal* under Denry's name. It began:

The recent robbery at Sneyd Hall gives us a reason to remember the beautiful paintings and furniture which it contains and which, happily, were not stolen. Only friends of the family, of course, ever see the great ballroom, but perhaps readers

Denry spent that long afternoon in the ballroom of Sneyd Hall, looking at pictures and furniture.

of the Signal *will be interested to read a description of this fine room . . .*

Everybody read the report of course, and everybody understood that Denry, who had already danced with the Countess, was now a good friend of the family.

*   *   *

The Savings Club was a great success; in fact, it became *too* successful. The reason was this. When customers had paid in two pounds, they were allowed to spend four pounds in the shops. They did spend four pounds in the shops. And Denry had to pay the shops. Customers were still paying in their five pence and their ten pence – but that wasn't enough to help Denry. His two thousand pounds in the bank was going very quickly. And then a whisper began to go round that Denry's famous Savings Club was not healthy, that it was going to fail, and that everyone would lose their money.

Denry knew that he had to do something – and do it very quickly. He thought of the Countess.

The Countess was very good at opening things. She opened hospitals and schools all over the Five Towns, and Denry read in the *Signal* that she was going to open a new Police Club in Hanbridge in a week's time. There are a number of facts about what happened on the day of the opening, and during the week before it. Some people may have ideas to explain some of these facts.

The facts are these. First: Denry called one day at the house of Mrs Kemp in Brougham Street. Mrs Kemp was the mother of Jock, Denry's old friend and carriage-driver to the Countess. Second: a day or two later, Jock came to visit his mother, and Denry also came to visit. Denry and Jock went for a short walk together. Third: on the afternoon of the opening of the Police Club, the Countess's carriage broke a wheel between Sneyd Hall and Hanbridge, about five kilometres from Hanbridge. Fourth: about five minutes later, Denry drove past in his mule cart, wearing his best clothes. Fifth: as Denry drove past, Jock called out, 'Excuse me, sir!' and Denry stopped. These are the facts.

'Good afternoon, Countess,' said Denry, lifting his hat.

'Oh, it's you, is it?' said the Countess. 'Good afternoon.'

'I see you've had an accident,' said Denry. 'Are you going somewhere important?'

'Yes, I *am* going somewhere important! I've got to be at the Police Club by three. And I shan't be. I'm late now.'

'I can get you there by three o'clock,' said Denry.

It was five kilometres to Hanbridge, and they were there in seventeen minutes. The mule was moving as fast as he could, but when they came into the main square, he stopped suddenly. There were several hundred policemen outside the Police Club, waiting for the Countess.

'Oh dear!' said Denry. 'He hates policemen.'

'I'll walk,' said the Countess.

'Oh no,' said Denry. 'It's all right.' He hit the mule over the head with his whip. The mule dashed off, but away from the Police Club. They hit another cart, full of vegetables, and turned it over. They dashed down a hill, fast. Then the Countess noticed that Denry was not using his right arm.

'I think I broke it when we hit the cart,' he said. 'Don't worry. I'll go up this hill – that'll stop him.'

Denry managed to turn the mule into Birches Street, which went up a hill. The mule slowed down, then stopped.

'Shall I drive him to the Club?' asked the Countess. She could see that Denry's arm was very painful.

And so the Countess arrived at the Police Club in Denry's

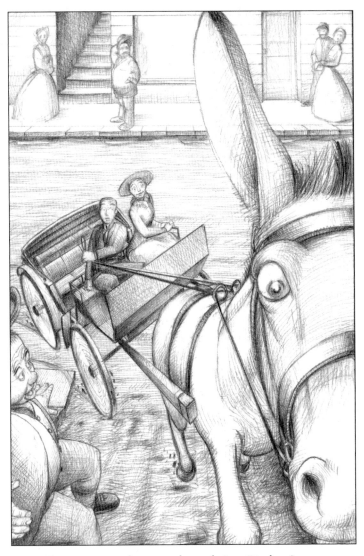

Denry managed to turn the mule into Birches Street.

mule cart. And she invited Denry to the Club opening, where she told the five mayors and all the important people of the Five Towns how Denry had rescued her.

After the opening, Denry left the Club with the Countess, to help her find her carriage. But it still had not arrived.

'I can take you home in my cart,' offered Denry.

'I think I'll wait,' said the Countess.

'Well, let's go and have a cup of tea while we're waiting,' said Denry. 'There's a good tea-shop near here.'

The Countess loved tea, and they were soon sitting in a corner of the tea-shop. The Countess looked hard at Denry.

'How did you get all that information about the rooms at Sneyd Hall?' she asked.

After this, the conversation became exciting.

That evening a notice appeared in the *Signal* which said that the Countess was now Patron of the Five Towns Savings Club. In a few days a thousand more people had joined the Club. Denry had no more worries about money.

6

THE BATTLE WITH DENRY'S MOTHER

Late one winter's evening a few years later, Denry opened the door of his mother's house in Brougham Street.

'Is that you, Denry?' came a tired voice.

'Yes,' he said, walking into the living room.

His mother was sitting very near the fire, which was burning brightly. She looked cold and ill.

'You must see a doctor, mother.'

'A doctor! What for? I've just got a bit of a cold, that's all.'

'You've been ill a lot this winter,' said Denry. 'It's this awful old house we live in.'

'It's a very good house. It was good enough for your father and it's good enough for me.'

'Mother, I'm earning two thousand pounds a year! And here we are, living in an old house at a rent of twenty-three pence a week!'

Actually, Denry was making nearly four thousand a year, but he was afraid to tell his mother that. These days he was a great man in the Five Towns, but his greatness was nothing in Brougham Street.

'You can go and live in a fine, grand house if you like, Denry,' said his mother. 'But I'm staying here.'

And so the battle went on. Denry wanted to move, but his

mother refused to leave Brougham Street. And Denry wouldn't move to a new house without her.

One morning a few weeks later, there was a letter for Mrs Machin from the man who owned her house. He had sold the house, he wrote, to a man in London, a Mr Wilbraham. From next month Mrs Machin must pay her rent to him.

The next day Denry came home with some news.

'I've met Mr Wilbraham, the man who bought our house. He came down from London. He wants me to collect the rents for him.'

'What did you tell him?'

'I said yes. Why not? It's easier for you. And he's an interesting man. He's building a new house up at Bleakridge. It's going to be a really modern house; a house where you can live comfortably without servants.'

'He's certainly a sensible man,' answered Mrs Machin. She hated servants and said so about once a week.

The house at Bleakridge started to grow. Mr Wilbraham stayed in London. The builder was Mr Cotterill (Denry had been friendly with the family since Llandudno), but Denry also kept an eye on things. The house was nearly finished when Mrs Machin got a second letter from Mr Wilbraham.

'He says we have to leave,' she cried. 'He wants us out immediately. Oh Denry, what shall we do!'

'We'll go and see him,' said Denry. 'He's coming to his new house tonight!'

So they put on their best clothes and went up to Bleakridge. Half an hour later they were standing outside Mr Wilbraham's house. Denry rang the bell, and they waited.

'Dirty doorstep,' said Mrs Machin, looking down at it. In Brougham Street it was important to have a clean doorstep, even if your rent *was* only twenty-three pence a week.

'Easy to clean,' said Denry. 'Watch!' He turned a tap next to the doorstep, and water ran over the step, washing it.

'Is that hot water?' asked Mrs Machin.

'Of course,' said Denry. He could see his mother liked the tap. 'Wilbraham's fixed a lot of things like that in his house.'

He rang again but there was no answer. 'Perhaps his train's late. I've got a key. We'll go in and wait for him.' He opened the door and turned on the electric light. Mrs Machin had never seen electric light before. She thought it was wonderful.

'It's very warm in here,' she said.

'Central heating,' said Denry. 'No fires to light, no wood to carry, no fireplaces to clean—'

The doorbell rang.

'There he is!' said Denry, moving to the door.

Three people stood on the washed doorstep – Mr and Mrs Cotterill, and Nellie. Mr Wilbraham had invited them, said Mr Cotterill.

'Oh, come in, come in!' said Denry. 'He's not here. Perhaps he's missed his train. But the house is all ready for him. Come on, I'll show you round.'

He and Nellie ran upstairs and the others followed. Upstairs the house was as wonderful as downstairs. So easy to clean. No work at all. 'Why,' said Mrs Cotterill, 'I could live here without any servants and still have it clean and tidy by ten o'clock in the morning.'

Mrs Machin had never seen electric light before.

Mrs Machin agreed.

Downstairs they found a fine cold supper ready to eat.

'Come on,' said Denry. 'Let's eat. I'm sure he'd like us to.'

Mrs Machin didn't want to. 'It's very strange that he isn't here,' she said.

'He's a strange man,' said Denry. 'I think he's a little mad.'

'I don't think he can be mad,' said Mrs Machin. 'The house is much too sensible for a madman.'

Finally, they all sat down to supper, and after some food and three bottles of wine they started to enjoy themselves. Soon Denry was searching the house for a fourth bottle of wine. He found one, opened it, drank some, and, with a cry, dropped the glass on the floor, where it broke.

It was not wine. It was a bottle of cleaning liquid. And the word POISON was written on it in large letters. Nellie didn't seem to realize how serious it was, and began to laugh.

47

Mrs Machin took Denry's arm. 'Come out to the kitchen,' she said. 'You must have some salt water, to make you sick.'

'Oh no!' said Denry. 'I'll be all right.'

But his mother wouldn't listen to him, and pulled him out of the room. Nellie had her hand over her mouth, trying very hard not to laugh, but not succeeding.

Ten minutes later they returned. Denry looked very white, and very cross. 'There's no danger now,' said Mrs Machin.

So the party came to an end. The Cotterills stood up to leave, and asked Denry how he was feeling.

'I feel much too ill to walk home,' he said. 'I'll sleep here. The bedrooms are all ready. My mother can stay too.'

The Cotterills left and Denry went to bed. After an hour his mother went to bed, too, but she slept very badly.

The next morning she was up before Denry and went out. Half an hour later she was back, waking Denry up.

'Oh, Denry! I've just been back home. They're pulling the house down. The roof's gone and the furniture . . .'

Denry sat up.

'I'll tell you something now,' he said. 'Wilbraham's dead.'

'Dead!'

'Dead. Well, he was never really alive, of course.'

And Mrs Machin understood. This was all Denry's plan to move her out of Brougham Street and up to Bleakridge. Soon all Bursley knew that Denry had won the battle with his mother. And they loved it.

But at least Mrs Machin had won with the salt water.

THE MAYOR, THE WIFE,
AND THE FOOTBALL CLUB

Soon after the move to Bleakridge, Bursley made Denry a Town Councillor. He was the youngest Councillor in the town, and one of the richest men in the Five Towns, but Councillor Cotterill still called him 'young man'.

Denry did not like Councillor Cotterill, but he was very friendly with Nellie and her mother. So when he bought one of the first cars in the Five Towns, he decided to invite them to go for a drive. When he got there, Nellie came to the door.

'Come in,' she said. 'I've got a surprise for you.'

In the sitting room, next to Mrs Cotterill, Denry saw a wonderful woman, beautifully dressed in black. When she turned to look at him, Denry suddenly recognized her. It was Ruth. Then he remembered that Ruth had married a rich man, a Mr Capron-Smith, who had recently died.

'Well, Denry,' she said, softly.

'Well, Ruth.'

Conversation was not difficult. Ruth was talking about a holiday in Switzerland. Denry listened with interest.

After a few minutes, the front door opened, and Mr Cotterill was heard in the hall. He did not come into the sitting room, so Mrs Cotterill went out to speak to him. When she came back, she was crying.

'It's the bank!' she cried. 'After all these years, and now, suddenly . . . all his money . . .'

Nellie and Ruth ran to her, and Denry decided it was probably better to leave. But as he walked into the hall, he met Councillor Cotterill. He was looking very worried.

'Ah, Denry,' he said. 'You're a friend of the family. We've no secrets from you. I'm afraid things are looking bad. The fact is, the bank wants its money and I can't pay.'

'What are you going to do?' asked Denry.

'We'll all go to Canada. My brother lives there – he's in the building business. He'll give me a job. It's stupid really. I only need two thousand pounds, for a month or two, until I sell the houses I'm building. I say,' he continued, 'you don't have a thousand or two, do you, young man? There'll be an excellent profit in two or three months. You and I have been friends for ten years.'

'And I suppose I've come to visit you once a fortnight,' answered Denry. 'Perhaps two hundred and fifty times in ten years. That's eight pounds a visit, Cotterill. That's more expensive than the most fashionable doctor in England!'

This conversation does not make Denry look very kind. But Councillor Cotterill had called him 'young man' too many times.

Several weeks later the Cotterills left Bursley and took the train to Liverpool, where they would take the ship to Canada. On the day they left the Five Towns, Denry happened to meet Ruth in the street.

'Did you know they have the cheapest tickets for the ship?' she said. 'It's terrible! And it's too late to change them now.'

'No, it isn't,' said Denry. 'I could go to Liverpool and arrange it. The ship doesn't leave until tomorrow.'

'Let's both go!' she said. 'And we'll pay half each for their new tickets.'

They had a very pleasant train journey. Ruth was warm and friendly to Denry, and as the train pulled into Liverpool, he had a very strange thought. 'I could still marry her! She's a fine woman, and now she's rich herself . . .'

They found the Cotterills, and paid for them to travel in a more comfortable part of the ship. Mr Cotterill said he would repay them, Mrs Cotterill cried, and Nellie said nothing at all. The ship's bell rang for the second time. Denry and Ruth said their goodbyes and started to leave.

Then Denry looked back and saw Nellie's sad little face. He felt as he had never felt before in his life. He wondered what was happening to his legs. He turned and ran back to Nellie.

'Look here,' he whispered. 'Come with me for a moment. There's something I want to give you. I left it in the taxi.'

Ruth was already lost in the crowds of people leaving the ship.

'But there's not time. The bell—'

'It'll only take a minute. Quick.' Without waiting to argue, he took her hand, pulled her off the ship, and towards a taxi.

'Which taxi is yours?' asked Nellie.

'Any one. It doesn't matter. Jump in.' He pushed her in.

'I'll miss the boat.'

'I know you will. I don't want you to go to Canada.'

Denry looked back and saw Nellie's sad little face.

'What are you going to do with me?' whispered Nellie.

'Well, what do you think?' shouted Denry. 'I'm going to marry you, of course!'

*   *   *

One evening Councillor Denry Machin sat down to tea with his wife, Nellie, in the house in Bleakridge. He opened the newspaper and read aloud: *Sudden Death of Councillor Bloor.*

'Poor man!' said Nellie. 'And he was going to be mayor in November, wasn't he?'

'So he was,' said Denry.

'Who'll be mayor now?'

'Barlow, I suppose,' said Denry.

'Barlow! He's an awful man! Nobody likes Barlow. Why don't they make you mayor?'

'Would you like to be mayoress?'

'I don't know. Why not?'

'I probably will be mayor after Barlow. But I want to be the youngest mayor, which means I'll have to do it this year, while I'm still thirty-three.'

'Who decides?'

'The Council, of course. But you're right. Nobody likes Barlow. And he's having a lot of problems with the Football Club. He's the chairman, you know.'

Bursley Football Club was having a very bad year. In fact it had had several very bad years. It lost most of its games, and because not many people wanted to see Bursley lose, few people went to watch the games.

A few days after Denry's conversation with Nellie there was

53

a crowded meeting at the Town Hall to discuss the club's future. Barlow, the chairman, got up to speak.

'I've been chairman of this club for thirteen years. In that time I've put two thousand pounds of my own money into the club. I can't put in any more. But what have you, the people of Bursley, done for your club? You don't come and watch. If we lose a game you stay at home the next week. We lose fifty or sixty pounds every time we play, and we can't go on like this.'

Several other people stood up to speak. Most of them had nothing kind to say about Councillor Barlow. All of them said that the club needed new players.

'New players!' said Barlow. 'Where's the money for new players? Has anybody got a thousand pounds?'

Nobody offered money. But more speakers stood up to ask for new players. Finally a man at the back of the hall stood up and walked up to the front.

'It's Machin!' said somebody. 'Good old Machin!'

Denry turned and looked at the sea of faces.

'I don't know a lot about football,' he said, 'although I enjoy a good game. But I do want to say something about new players. Isn't it true that one of the best players in England comes from Bursley?'

'Yes!' shouted the crowd. 'Callear! He's the best player in England!'

'That's right. Callear. He left Bursley when he was nineteen to play for Liverpool. He scored a lot of goals there in three years. Then he went to York, didn't he? And York have some money problems now, I hear, and want to sell some of their players.

Gentlemen, Callear must come back home to Bursley.'

The crowd in the hall were now very noisy and excited. Barlow jumped angrily to his feet.

'And how are we going to get Callear? Councillor Machin says he doesn't know much about football, and it's true! Aston Villa have already offered £700 for Callear. Blackburn have offered £750. Has anybody here got £800?'

'Have you finished?' asked Denry, who was still standing.

The hall exploded with laughter.

'Have you finished?' asked Denry.

'Now,' called Denry, 'Mr Callear, will you please come up to the front of the hall?'

The hall was suddenly silent. A tall young man walked nervously down to the front of the hall.

'That's him!' said somebody. 'It's Callear. Good old Callear! Good old Machin!'

'Well?' asked Denry, turning to Barlow. 'Do you want him?'

'Yes. But what about the money?'

'That's my problem. I've just come back from York. If you want him, you can have him.'

Two days later a letter appeared in the *Signal*. It said that Denry should be the next mayor. Other letters followed, saying the same thing, and that Bursley needed a young and popular mayor. And when the Council met, it agreed.

That evening Denry told Nellie: 'You'll be the mayoress to the youngest mayor. And it's cost me, with hotels and travel, about eight hundred and eleven pounds!'

After the meeting a group of councillors were talking about Denry.

'What a card!' said one, laughing.

'There's never been a man like him in all the Five Towns!' said another.

'But he's never done a day's work in his life,' said Barlow. 'What's he done for the town?'

'What's he done? He's made us all laugh! That's what he's done.'

GLOSSARY

advertisement a notice (e.g. in a newspaper) which tells people about jobs, things to sell, etc.

ball a big party where people dance

brake *(n)* something that you use to stop a moving car or cart

canal a kind of river, made by people, where boats can travel

card *(old-fashioned)* an unusual and amusing person

carriage a kind of 'car', pulled by horses, used for carrying people

cart a wooden 'car', with two or four wheels, pulled by a horse

chairman a person who controls a meeting

cheerful looking or sounding happy

club a group of people with the same interests, and the building where they meet

collect to go and bring something from a place

Council a group of people (Councillors) who are chosen to work together to decide things for a town or city

countess a title for a woman from an important family

dash to run quickly; to hurry

earn to get money by working

engaged having agreed to marry someone

examination a test of what you know or can do

fan a thing that moves the air to make you cooler

fellow a friendly word for a man

lawyer someone whose job is helping people with the law

lifeboat a boat that helps people who are in danger at sea

liquid water, oil, and milk are liquids

mad with a sick mind

mayor the leader of a Town or City Council

millionaire   a person who has more than a million pounds

mule   an animal whose parents were a horse and a donkey

patron   a famous person who uses their name or money to help people

pick up   to learn quickly

pier   a long platform built from the land into the sea, where people can walk or get on or off boats

poison   something that will kill you or make you very ill if you eat or drink it

pottery   pots, dishes, plates, etc. made with clay and baked in a very hot fire

profit   money that you get when you sell something for more than it cost to buy or make

property   a building and the land around it

rent *(v and n)*   to pay somebody money to use a house, shop, etc.

rescue *(n)*   saving or bringing someone away from danger

row *(v)*   to move a boat through water using oars (long pieces of wood with flat ends)

servant   someone who works in another person's house

souvenir   something you keep to remember a place

tap   a thing that you turn to let water come out of a pipe

tax   money you pay to the council, to pay for roads, hospitals, etc.

town hall   a building with offices for the Council and rooms for meetings, dances, etc.

trip *(n)*   a journey

van   a covered lorry for carrying things

whip   a long thin thing used for hitting animals

widow   a woman whose husband has died

wine   an alcoholic drink made from grapes

wreck *(n)*   a ship that has been badly damaged in an accident

The Card

ACTIVITIES

Before Reading

1 **Read the story introduction on the first page of the book, and the back cover. Which of these words do you think will describe Denry? Circle Y (Yes), N (No), or P (Perhaps) for each one.**

clever Y/N/P	unlucky Y/N/P	polite Y/N/P
happy Y/N/P	miserable Y/N/P	funny Y/N/P
quiet Y/N/P	good-looking Y/N/P	honest Y/N/P
brave Y/N/P	hard-working Y/N/P	kind Y/N/P

2 **How does Denry do it? Can you guess? Choose one answer for each question.**

1 How does he get an invitation to the ball?

   a) He buys one.

   b) He puts his own name on the list.

   c) He writes one to himself.

2 How does he become Mrs Codleyn's rent-collector?

   a) He does it at night, working under a different name.

   b) He marries Mrs Codleyn.

   c) He offers to do the job more cheaply than anyone else.

3 How does he make a thousand pounds from the *Hjalmar?*

   a) He sells tickets for a trip to see the ship.

   b) He buys the ship and sells it again.

   c) He puts the ship onto land and makes it into a hotel.

While Reading

Read Chapter 1. Choose the best question-word for these questions, and then answer them.

What / Why

1 . . . did Mrs Machin call her son Denry?
2 . . . did Denry do to his mark in the examination?
3 . . . did Mr Duncalf give Denry a job?
4 . . . did Denry need to do before he went to the ball?
5 . . . did Denry decide to ask the Countess to dance?
6 . . . question did Denry refuse to answer?
7 . . . did Denry do as the Countess was leaving?

Before you read Chapter 2, can you guess who will make trouble for Denry?

1 The Countess   2 Mr Duncalf   3 Ruth   4 Harold Etches

Read Chapter 2. Are these sentences true (T) or false (F)?

1 Mrs Codleyn never paid the taxes on her houses.
2 Denry lied to Mr Duncalf about his invitation to the ball.
3 Denry was not worried when he lost his job.
4 Denry began lending money to help people pay their rent.
5 Widow Hullins couldn't pay her rent so Denry made her a present of the house.

Before you read Chapter 3 (*The dancing teacher and the furniture van*), how do you think the chapter gets its name?

1 Ruth buys a furniture van and joins Denry in business.
2 Denry offers to move Ruth's furniture, but has an accident with the van.
3 Ruth can't pay her rent and tries to run away, but the van carrying her furniture falls into the canal.

Read Chapter 4, then match these halves of sentences.

1 Although Denry was happy to be engaged to Ruth, . . .
2 Nellie offered to pay for things at Llandudno, . . .
3 Then the engagement ended . . .
4 After Denry bought the old lifeboat . . .
5 When Denry met the Cotterills on the beach . . .
6 Finally, he sold the lifeboat . . .
7 he invited them to dinner at an expensive hotel.
8 he found it was very expensive.
9 and took a hatbox full of money home to his mother.
10 but Denry wouldn't let her.
11 he sold boat trips to the wreck and made a lot of money.
12 when Denry called himself 'Rothschild' at the bookshop.

Before you read Chapter 5 (*The rescue of the Countess*), can you guess what Denry rescues the Countess from?

1 a fire   3 a thief
2 an accident on the road   4 the canal

Read Chapter 5. Then answer these questions.

Who

1 . . . did Denry want as patron of his Savings Club?
2 . . . drove the Countess's carriage?
3 . . . wrote a report about Sneyd Hall for the *Signal*?
4 . . . was going to open the new Police Club?
5 . . . were waiting outside the Police Club?
6 . . . broke his arm when the mule hit another cart?
7 . . . had a cup of tea in a teashop near the Town Hall?

Before you read Chapter 6 (*The battle with Denry's mother*), can you guess what the battle will be about?

1 money   3 a new house
2 Denry's job   4 Denry's wife

Read Chapter 7 as far as the bottom of page 50. How do you think the story will end? Choose some of these ideas.

1 Denry marries Ruth.
2 Denry marries Nellie.
3 Denry goes to Canada with the Cotterills.
4 Denry comes back from Canada with lots of money.
5 Denry becomes the youngest mayor Bursley has ever had.
6 Denry is asked to be mayor, but says no.
7 Denry makes a lot of money when the Football Club wins.
8 Denry buys a very good player for the Football Club.
9 Ruth uses her money to save the Football Club.

After Reading

1 **What did you think of the things Denry did? Were they good or bad? Put a mark in each box, from 1 (very bad) to 10 (very good). Explain why you have chosen each mark.**

- changing his mark in the examination ☐
- getting invitations to the ball for himself, Ruth, and young Shillitoe ☐
- taking Harold Etches' five pounds after dancing with the Countess ☐
- taking Mrs Codleyn's rent-collecting business ☐
- lending money to make more money ☐
- giving Widow Hullins her house ☐
- rescuing Ruth and not telling anyone about her money problems ☐
- not paying for Ruth to stay on in Llandudno ☐
- saying his name was 'Rothschild' ☐
- writing about Sneyd Hall for the *Signal* ☐
- planning the Countess's 'accident' with Jock ☐
- rescuing the Countess after the 'accident' ☐
- lying to his mother about the new house ☐
- not helping Councillor Cotterill with his money problems ☐
- taking Nellie off the ship to Canada ☐
- buying Callear for Bursley Football Club ☐

ie Countess say to each other in the
ersation in the right order, and write in
e Countess speaks first (number 4).

ie window! But that was later. First, I
hoping somebody would come.'
ou write that piece for the *Signal*?'
v did that happen?'
ft all that information about the
?'

noon looking at everything. When it
indow and went home.'
ed breaking windows . . .'
i a question, but I got locked in the

_____ ....u now you want me to help you, I suppose. So
what was this question you wanted to ask me . . .?'

9 _____ 'I thought I was very lucky to spend a day among all
those lovely things. I thought people would like to know
about them.'

10 _____ 'But nobody came. So what did you do?'

11 _____ 'Lucky Mr Machin, eh? And this afternoon, when
you rescued me – that was lucky too?'

12 _____ 'I was following one of the servants, but I lost him.
And when I tried to find my way out, all the doors were
locked.'

13 _____ 'Yes, it was, wasn't it? And I was happy to help.'

3 There are 23 words (3 letters or longer) from the story in this word search. Find the words and draw lines through them. They go from left to right, and from top to bottom.

E	X	A	M	I	N	A	T	I	O	N	I	L	F
N	P	R	O	P	E	R	T	Y	Y	T	R	I	P
G	T	A	X	W	O	L	U	W	A	N	E	S	C
A	D	V	E	R	T	I	S	E	M	E	N	T	H
G	T	A	H	E	I	Q	P	M	A	M	T	Y	E
E	O	N	C	C	U	U	O	A	Y	R	C	A	E
D	B	R	A	K	E	I	I	R	O	O	N	H	R
M	W	I	N	E	A	D	S	K	R	W	V	E	F
A	H	T	A	P	I	C	O	L	L	E	C	T	U
D	M	I	L	L	I	O	N	A	I	R	E	M	L

4 Look at the word search again and write down all the letters that don't have a line through them. Begin with the first line and go across each line to the end. You should have 25 letters, which will make a sentence of 8 words.

1 What are the words, and who said them?
2 Where was he, and who was he talking about?
3 What big change happened in his life after this?

5 Here are the people of Bursley talking about Denry. Say what the speakers are talking about, and then put the six pieces of news in the right order for the story.

1 'Yes, it's true. It belongs to her now – and she didn't have

to pay him a penny for it. Isn't that extraordinary? It was just a funny idea at first – but then he did it!'

2 'It's the best thing that's happened to the Club for years. And Barlow's face! You had to laugh. Well, I think I know the name of our next mayor – and it doesn't start with B.'

3 'Doesn't he write well! It's like being there and seeing it yourself – all those beautiful paintings . . . You can tell he goes there a lot. I'm sure he's a great friend of the family.'

4 'No, nobody had any idea! Of course, he's known the family for years, but nobody guessed. And suddenly there they are, back from Liverpool, smiling all over their faces!'

5 'Just like that! Well, she said yes – I couldn't believe it. And he said something that made her laugh and laugh – but nobody knows what it was. He just won't say.'

6 'Yes, all over the floor – hundreds of them. She's still finding them in corners and under the furniture. And what did she say? Not a word! That's the biggest surprise!'

6 **What did you think about this story and its characters? Complete some of these sentences.**

1 I liked _____ *best / least* because _____.

2 The part of the story I enjoyed *most / least* was _____.

3 I *would / wouldn't* like Denry as my *husband / friend / rent-collector* because _____.

4 I think Denry would make a *good / bad* mayor for Bursley because _____.

ABOUT THE AUTHOR

Arnold Bennett was born in 1867 in Hanley, Staffordshire. His father was a solicitor, who wanted his son to be a solicitor too. But when Bennett was twenty-one, he went to London and worked in an office while he was trying to become a writer. In 1893 he got a job on a famous magazine for women, and his first novel, *A Man from the North*, came out in 1898.

From 1902 to 1912 he lived in Paris, and he married a Frenchwoman, but the marriage did not last. He wrote a huge number of books, short stories, articles, journals, and practical books about writing. Some of his most famous novels are *Anna of the Five Towns, The Old Wives' Tale, Clayhanger,* and *Riceyman Steps*. He also loved the theatre and wrote some very successful plays. He died in 1931.

Like the French 'realist' writers, such as Flaubert and the Goncourt brothers, Bennett wanted to write about the real lives of working people. So he wrote about everyday life in the 'Five Towns' of the English Midlands, which became famous in the 1800s for their pottery.

Bennett also wrote several lighter works, such as *The Card* (1911), which became one of his most popular books. In this novel he used his own experiences, such as rent-collecting for his father, and his memories of local characters. In fact, Bennett's friend H. K. Hales thought that he was the model for Denry, and years later he asked Bennett for some of the money from the book. If this was true, replied Bennett, Hales should pay *him* for the free advertising the book had given him. You can hear Denry's voice in the question – and in the answer.

OXFORD BOOKWORMS LIBRARY

Classics • Crime & Mystery • Factfiles • Fantasy & Horror
Human Interest • Playscripts • Thriller & Adventure
True Stories • World Stories

The OXFORD BOOKWORMS LIBRARY provides enjoyable reading in English, with a wide range of classic and modern fiction, non-fiction, and plays. It includes original and adapted texts in seven carefully graded language stages, which take learners from beginner to advanced level. An overview is given on the next pages.

All Stage 1 titles are available as audio recordings, as well as over eighty other titles from Starter to Stage 6. All Starters and many titles at Stages 1 to 4 are specially recommended for younger learners. Every Bookworm is illustrated, and Starters and Factfiles have full-colour illustrations.

The OXFORD BOOKWORMS LIBRARY also offers extensive support. Each book contains an introduction to the story, notes about the author, a glossary, and activities. Additional resources include tests and worksheets, and answers for these and for the activities in the books. There is advice on running a class library, using audio recordings, and the many ways of using Oxford Bookworms in reading programmes. Resource materials are available on the website <www.oup.com/elt/bookworms>.

The *Oxford Bookworms Collection* is a series for advanced learners. It consists of volumes of short stories by well-known authors, both classic and modern. Texts are not abridged or adapted in any way, but carefully selected to be accessible to the advanced student.

You can find details and a full list of titles in the *Oxford Bookworms Library Catalogue* and *Oxford English Language Teaching Catalogues*, and on the website <www.oup.com/elt/bookworms>.

THE OXFORD BOOKWORMS LIBRARY
GRADING AND SAMPLE EXTRACTS

STARTER • 250 HEADWORDS

present simple – present continuous – imperative –
can/cannot, must – *going to* (future) – simple gerunds …

Her phone is ringing – but where is it?

Sally gets out of bed and looks in her bag. No phone. She looks under the bed. No phone. Then she looks behind the door. There is her phone. Sally picks up her phone and answers it. *Sally's Phone*

STAGE 1 • 400 HEADWORDS

… past simple – coordination with *and*, *but*, *or* –
subordination with *before*, *after*, *when*, *because*, *so* …

I knew him in Persia. He was a famous builder and I worked with him there. For a time I was his friend, but not for long. When he came to Paris, I came after him – I wanted to watch him. He was a very clever, very dangerous man. *The Phantom of the Opera*

STAGE 2 • 700 HEADWORDS

… present perfect – *will* (future) – *(don't) have to, must not, could* –
comparison of adjectives – simple *if* clauses – past continuous –
tag questions – *ask/tell* + infinitive …

While I was writing these words in my diary, I decided what to do. I must try to escape. I shall try to get down the wall outside. The window is high above the ground, but I have to try. I shall take some of the gold with me – if I escape, perhaps it will be helpful later. *Dracula*

... should, may – present perfect continuous – *used to* – past perfect –
causative – relative clauses – indirect statements ...

Of course, it was most important that no one should see
Colin, Mary, or Dickon entering the secret garden. So Colin
gave orders to the gardeners that they must all keep away
from that part of the garden in future. ***The Secret Garden***

STAGE 4 • 1400 HEADWORDS

... past perfect continuous – passive (simple forms) –
would conditional clauses – indirect questions –
relatives with *where/when* – gerunds after prepositions/phrases ...

I was glad. Now Hyde could not show his face to the world
again. If he did, every honest man in London would be proud
to report him to the police. ***Dr Jekyll and Mr Hyde***

STAGE 5 • 1800 HEADWORDS

... future continuous – future perfect –
passive (modals, continuous forms) –
would have conditional clauses – modals + perfect infinitive ...

If he had spoken Estella's name, I would have hit him. I was so
angry with him, and so depressed about my future, that I could
not eat the breakfast. Instead I went straight to the old house.
Great Expectations

STAGE 6 • 2500 HEADWORDS

... passive (infinitives, gerunds) – advanced modal meanings –
clauses of concession, condition

When I stepped up to the piano, I was confident. It was as if I
knew that the prodigy side of me really did exist. And when I
started to play, I was so caught up in how lovely I looked that
I didn't worry how I would sound. ***The Joy Luck Club***

Love Story

ERICH SEGAL

Retold by Rosemary Border

This is a love story you won't forget. Oliver Barrett meets Jenny Cavilleri. He plays sports, she plays music. He's rich, and she's poor. They argue, and they fight, and they fall in love.

So they get married, and make a home together. They work hard, they enjoy life, they make plans for the future. Then they learn that they don't have much time left.

Their story has made people laugh, and cry, all over the world.

A Christmas Carol

CHARLES DICKENS

Retold by Clare West

Christmas is humbug, Scrooge says – just a time when you find yourself a year older and not a penny richer. The only thing that matters to Scrooge is business, and making money.

But on Christmas Eve three spirits come to visit him. They take him travelling on the wings of the night to see the shadows of Christmas past, present, and future – and Scrooge learns a lesson that he will never forget.